The Earth's moon is quite big too; it is about a quarter of the size of the Earth.

Earth's moon

(Names can be confusing: *a moon* orbits a planet, but '*the Moon*' is the name we give to the moon that orbits planet Earth.)

Moons orbit planets (and planets in our Solar System orbit the Sun) as a result of a force we call gravity. Gravity is a force that pulls things together.

It takes 28 days for the Moon to orbit the Earth.

The Moon has day and night like the Earth, but the days are much longer. A day on the Moon is as long as 27 days on Earth.

Planet Earth

Scientists think that the Moon was formed about four and a half billion years ago, when a huge rock as big as a planet crashed into the Earth.

When the huge rock broke up, most of it was blasted up into space. Some rocks from the Earth ended up in space too.

The Moon

Written by
David Orme

Moons are large natural objects in space that travel in an orbit around a planet. Our planet Earth has only one moon, but some planets have lots of them. The planet Jupiter has 67 moons, and astronomers may not have found all of them yet!

Most moons are much smaller than the planet they orbit. Jupiter is a large planet and has some very big moons. The biggest one is called Ganymede, and it is bigger than the planet Mercury.

The planet Jupiter

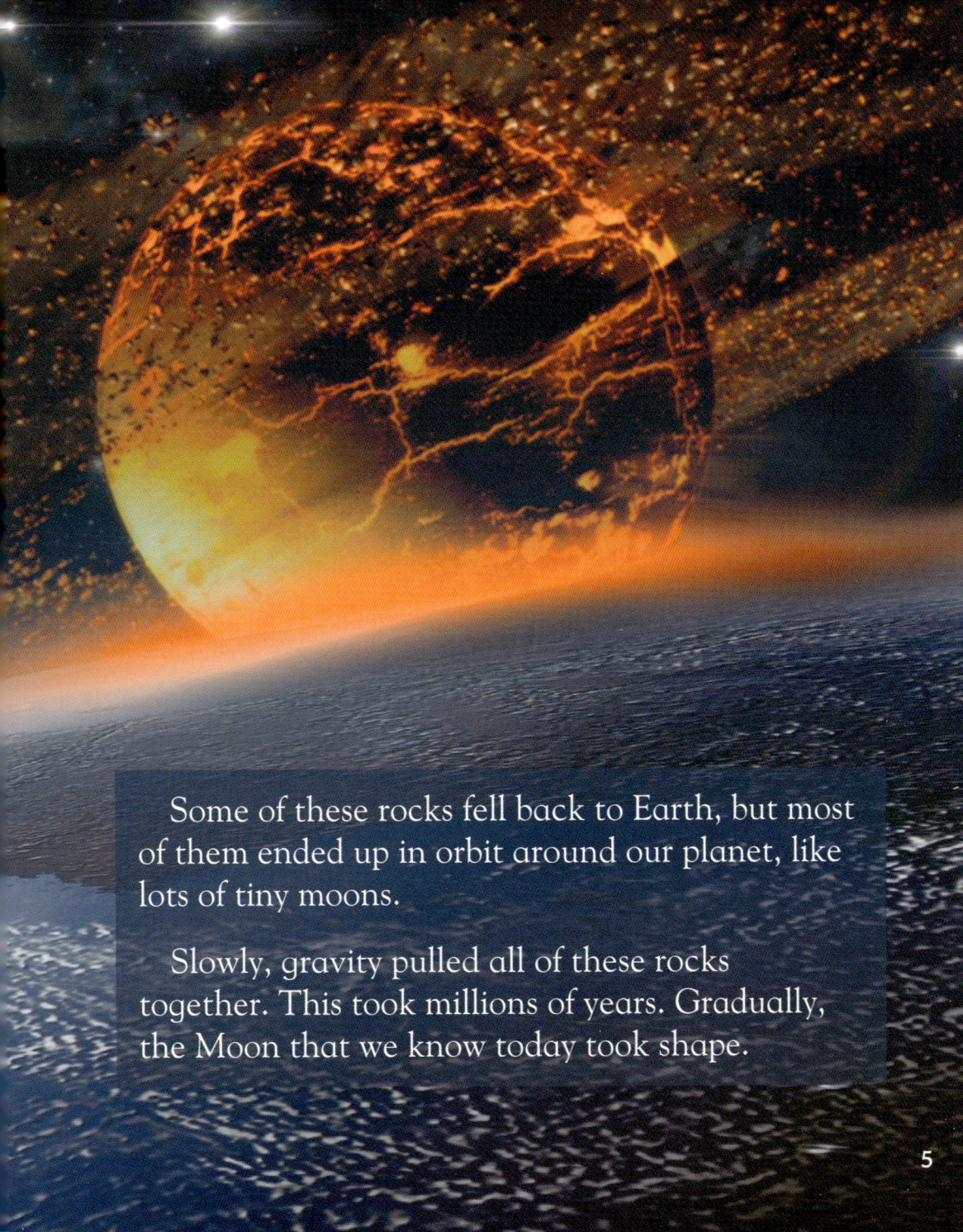

Some of these rocks fell back to Earth, but most of them ended up in orbit around our planet, like lots of tiny moons.

Slowly, gravity pulled all of these rocks together. This took millions of years. Gradually, the Moon that we know today took shape.

How does the Moon affect the Earth?

As the Moon moves around the Earth, its gravity pulls on the Earth.

This force isn't strong enough for us to notice. Your hair doesn't stand on end when the Moon is up above you!

The force does have an important effect on the Earth's oceans. As the Moon moves around the Earth, it pulls on the Earth's water; this creates tides.

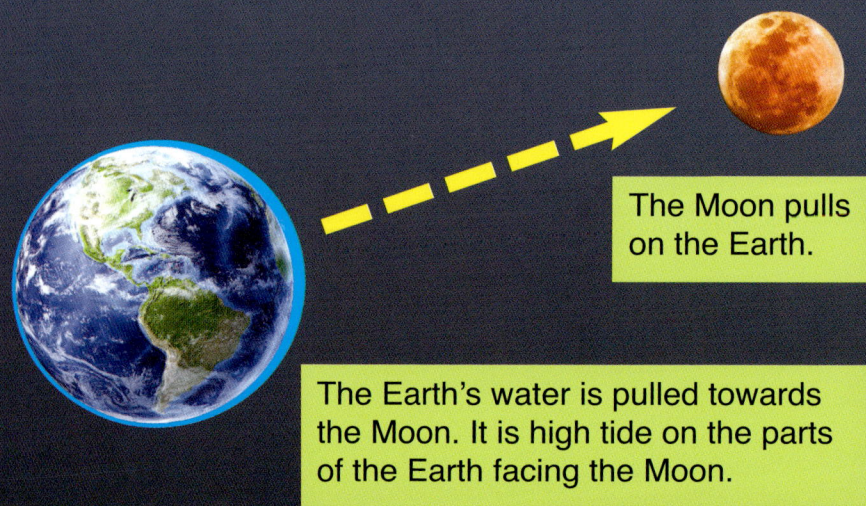

The Moon pulls on the Earth.

The Earth's water is pulled towards the Moon. It is high tide on the parts of the Earth facing the Moon.

The Sun pulls on the Earth's water in the same way.

When the Sun and the Moon are pulling together in the same direction, the movement of the Earth's tides is much greater. This is called a spring tide.

The Sun and Moon pull on the Earth.

The Earth's water is pulled harder. This is a spring tide.

Here is a beach at high tide and at low tide:

Why does the Moon seem to change shape in the sky?

When it is day on one side of the Earth, it is night on the other side. Day is when your part of the Earth faces the Sun. It is the same for the Moon.

When the Moon is between the Earth and the Sun, we see the side that is in the Sun's shadow, like this:

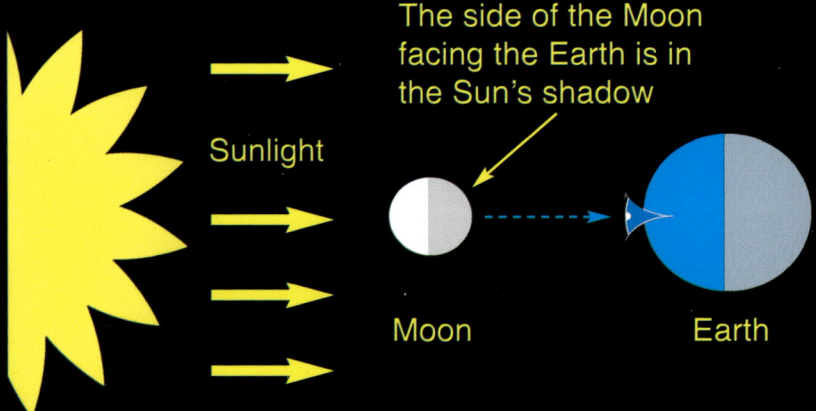

This is called a new Moon.

When the Earth is between the Sun and the Moon, we see all of its day side. This is a full Moon. Because it takes twenty-eight days for the Moon to go round the Earth, we see a full Moon every four weeks.

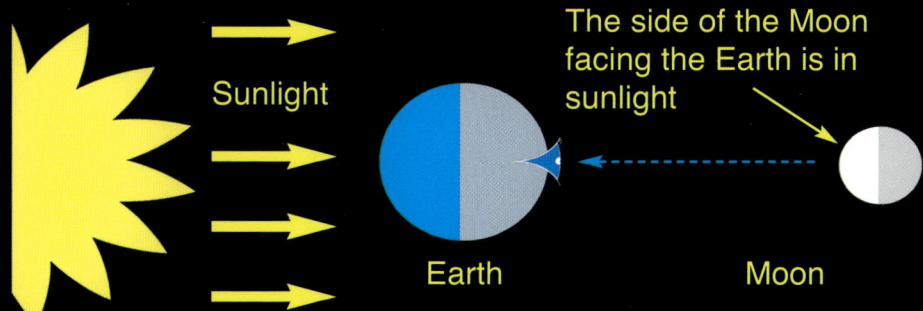

Between a new Moon and a full Moon, only a part of the Moon that we see is lit by the Sun, like this:

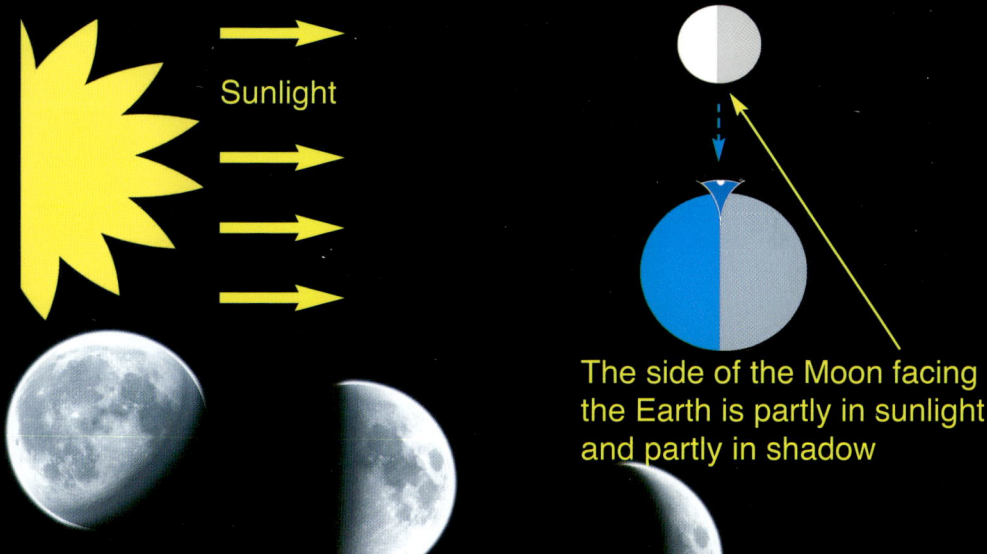

What is the surface of the Moon like?

The Moon isn't a comfortable place to be!

There is no atmosphere on the Moon. There is no air to breathe. It also means that at night it is much colder on the Moon than anywhere on Earth. During the daytime, it is much, much hotter.

The surface of the Moon is rough, rocky and dusty. In the past, the Moon had many volcanoes, and lava spread out over the surface to make flat plains. In the past, people thought these might be seas. They are the dark areas in this small picture.

Over millions of years, the Moon has been hit by many comets. These have made deep craters in the surface.

Comets have hit the Earth too, but the surface of the Earth has changed because of weather, so the craters have nearly all gone. Nothing has changed on the Moon for millions of years.

The first man on the Moon.

In 1969 the Apollo 11 mission landed on the Moon. Neil Armstrong was the first person to walk on the Moon, and Buzz Aldrin was the second. Back on the Earth, people were able to watch the Moonwalk on TV.

When Neil Armstrong stepped on to the Moon, he said, "It's one small step for man, one giant leap for mankind."

Neil Armstrong and Buzz Aldrin spent 21 hours on the Moon, but only about 2½ hours outside their lunar module. They gathered up rocks to take back to Earth, so that scientists could really find out what the Moon was made of.

They planted an American flag, but it fell over when they took off. They also left a footprint on the Moon!

Astronaut Buzz Aldrin on the Moon, 1969. Photograph taken by Neil Armstrong. (You can see Armstrong in the reflection in Aldrin's helmet visor.)

Exploring the Moon

After Apollo 11, there were five more landings on the Moon. These were by Apollo 12, Apollo 14, Apollo 15, Apollo 16 and Apollo 17.

Each mission landed on a different part of the Moon. This map shows where they landed.

Apollo missions: landing sites

Apollo 13 was going to land on the Moon, but the mission went wrong, and the astronauts only just managed to get back to Earth safely.

The last three missions stayed much longer on the Moon and had a moon buggy to help them collect interesting rocks.

Will we go back to the Moon?

Scientists would like to set up a base on the Moon where people could live. We now know that there is water on the Moon – this might make a Moon base possible.

The great mystery of the Moon

The same side of the Moon always faces the Earth. This means that, before space flight, no one knew what was on the other side of the Moon.

In 1959 a space probe went right round the Moon and took a photograph. The mystery was solved!

The far side of the Moon